Magnificent mane
 (though Uni's was *extra* magnificent).
Golden hooves
 (though Uni's were *extra* golden).

Amy Krouse Rosenthal

Uni the UNICORN

illustrated by Brigette Barrager

PUFFIN

*I*n almost every way,
Uni was like all the other unicorns.

Sparkling purple eyes
(though Uni's were *extra* sparkling).

Like the other unicorns,
    Uni had a special swirly horn
    with the power to heal and mend.

And like the
other unicorns,

Uni could make wishes come true.

But there was one thing
that definitely set Uni apart . . .

Fairy Tales

Little Girl Stories

LITTLE WOMEN

Uni believed that little girls were REAL.

Uni's friends laughed and said,
"Ha, ha, ha, silly Uni. Everyone knows
there's no such thing as little girls!
They're just make-believe!"

At home, Uni's parents
just brushed it off
with knowing smiles.

But Uni was certain, absolutely certain,
that little girls were real,
no matter what everyone else said.

Uni knew that somewhere far away
    (but not *that* far away),
    there was a little girl waiting . . .
    a strong, smart, wonderful, magical little girl.

And she would be the best friend
    a unicorn could ever ask for.

Uni imagined all the things
    they would do together . . .

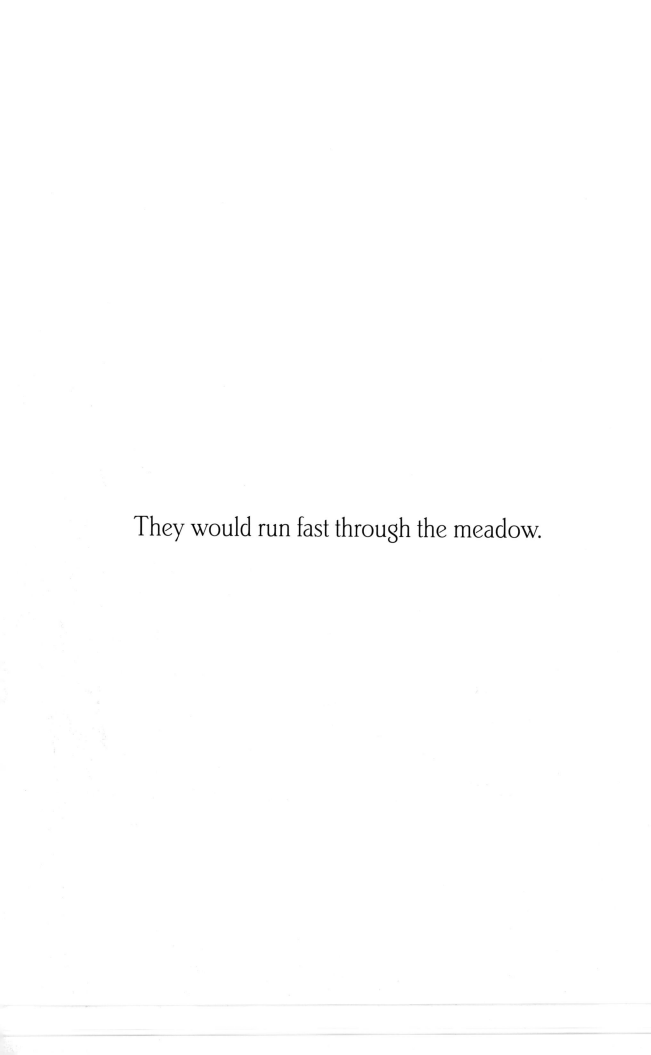

They would run fast through the meadow.

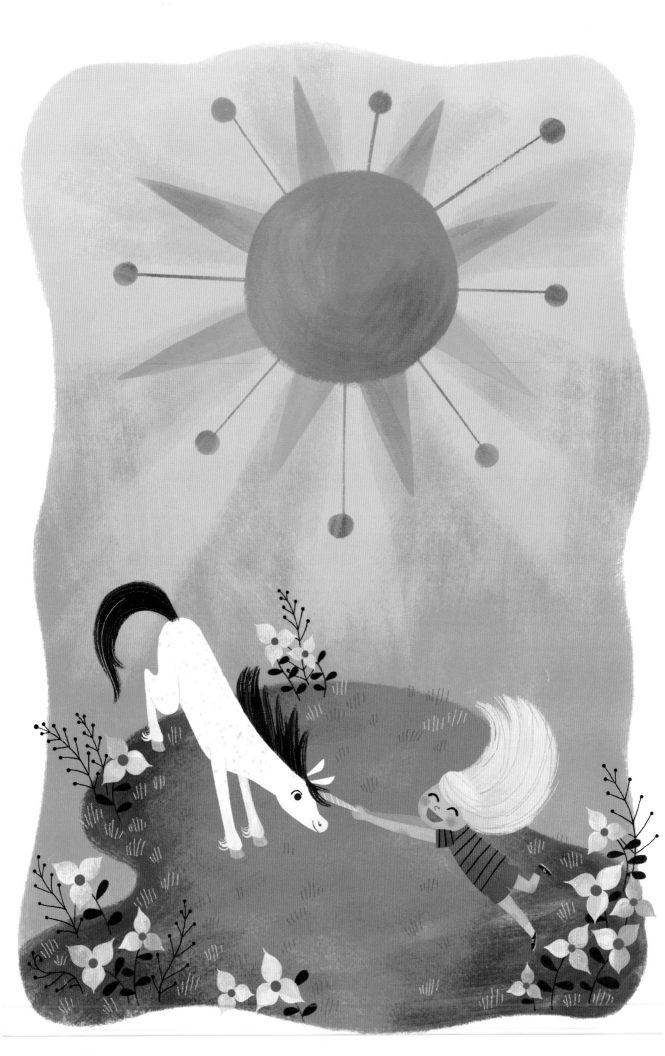

They would spin and twirl in the sunlight.

They would explore, and help
forest creatures in need.

Other times, they would just sit quietly
and talk about important things.

And of course of course of course

they would slide down rainbows together.

Uni fell asleep that night
and had enchanted dreams

What Uni did not yet know,
   but would discover soon enough,
   was that somewhere far away
   (but not *that* far away) . . .

   . . . there was indeed a real little girl.

And even though her friends said,
"Ha, ha, ha. Unicorns are just
make-believe!"

And despite her parents' knowing smiles . . .

. . . this little girl was certain, absolutely certain, that there was a unicorn, a strong, smart, wonderful, magical unicorn . . .

. . . just waiting to be her friend.